How do we measure matter?

by Lynn Peppas

🌳 Crabtree Publishing Company

www.crabtreebooks.com

Matter Close-Up

Author
Lynn Peppas

Publishing plan research and development
Sean Charlebois, Reagan Miller
Crabtree Publishing Company

Editors
Kathy Middleton
Reagan Miller

Proofreader
Wendy Scavuzzo

Photo research and graphic design
Katherine Berti

Print and production coordinator
Katherine Berti

Photographs
Dreamstime: page 3
Thinkstock: back cover, pages 17 (top right),
   19 (top)
Other images by Shutterstock

Library and Archives Canada Cataloguing in Publication

Peppas, Lynn
   How do we measure matter? / Lynn Peppas.

(Matter close-up)
Includes index.
Issued also in electronic format.
ISBN 978-0-7787-0768-4 (bound).--ISBN 978-0-7787-0775-2 (pbk.)

   1. Measurement--Juvenile literature. 2. Measuring instruments--
Juvenile literature. I. Title. II. Series: Matter close-up

QA465.P47 2012   j530.8   C2012-904365-6

Library of Congress Cataloging-in-Publication Data

CIP available at Library of Congress

Crabtree Publishing Company

www.crabtreebooks.com   1-800-387-7650

Printed in Hong Kong/092012/BK20120629

Published in Canada
Crabtree Publishing
616 Welland Ave.
St. Catharines, Ontario
L2M 5V6

Published in the United States
Crabtree Publishing
PMB 59051
350 Fifth Avenue, 59th Floor
New York, New York 10118

Published in the United Kingdom
Crabtree Publishing
Maritime House
Basin Road North, Hove
BN41 1WR

Published in Australia
Crabtree Publishing
3 Charles Street
Coburg North
VIC 3058

Contents

What is matter?

Matter is everything around us. Matter is anything that takes up space. All matter has **mass**. Mass is the amount of material or particles in matter. You measure matter to find out more about it.

All matter can be sorted into solids, liquids, and gases. Matter can be a solid such as Earth. It can be a liquid such as a lake. It can also be a gas such as the air we breathe.

What do you think?

Identify the states of matter in each picture on this page and the opposite page. Which pictures show all three states of matter?

Properties of matter that we measure

Solids, liquids, and gases have different **properties**. A property is a feature that something has. Properties help us describe, compare, and measure different types of matter.

Air is a gas. This outdoor thermometer tells you the temperature of the air outside. The temperature outside tells you what you need to wear.

For any solid, liquid, or gas, you can measure its weight and its mass, or the amount of material in it. You can also measure **temperature** and **volume**, which is the amount of space something takes up. For a solid, you can also measure its size to find its **height**, **width**, or **depth**.

Water and honey are liquids. They both can be poured. Water is thin and slippery. It pours quickly. Honey is thick and gooey. It pours slowly. Thick, thin, slippery, and gooey are properties. How fast a liquid pours is a property, too!

Measuring and collecting data

There are different ways to measure matter.

One way is to compare two things to each other.

Numbers can also be used to show an amount.

The measurements you collect are called **data**.

Measuring up

You can measure with tools such as a ruler. A measuring tool gives an amount to something that people everywhere can understand. If you do not have a measuring tool, you can also measure matter using everyday things. It will not give you an exact measure, but it will give you an idea of how big or heavy something is.

9

What do you think?

Which measuring tool—the bananas or the ruler—will tell your online friend in Mexico how tall your cat really is?

The cat is 6 bananas or about 10 inches (25 cm) tall.

He is taller and she is shorter. Comparing is a way to measure matter.

Units of measure

Almost every country in the world uses the **metric system** to measure amounts. The metric system uses meters to measure the size of a solid. It uses liters to measure the volume of liquids. Mass and weight is measured in grams. Temperatures are measured in degrees Celsius.

U.S. customary system

The **U.S. customary system** is used by people living in the United States to measure matter. This system measures the size of a solid in inches and feet. It uses ounces, cups, and gallons to measure the volume of liquids. Mass is measured in ounces and pounds. Temperatures are measured in degrees Fahrenheit.

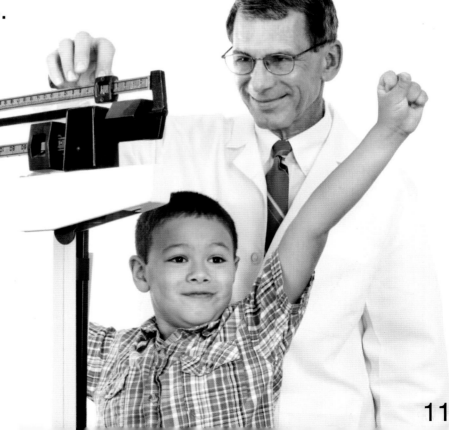

Measuring temperature

A thermometer is a tool that measures the temperature of different types of matter. Temperature is measured in degrees. Sometimes you will see a temperature recorded like this: 77° F (25° C). The small circle after the number is a **symbol** that means degree. The "F" means Fahrenheit, and the "C" means Celsius.

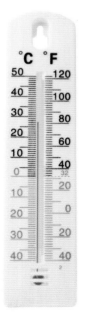

Some thermometers have arrows that point to the measurement of the temperature. Some have red or black liquid that rises or falls inside a thin tube to the correct amount of degrees. **Digital** thermometers show numbers only.

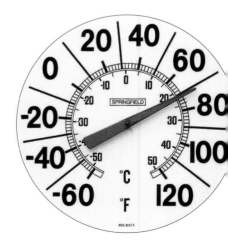

Different thermometers

An outdoor thermometer measures the temperature of the air. You can tell by the temperature how to dress for the day. Do you have a fever? A thermometer placed under your tongue tells an adult what temperature your body is. If your body temperature is higher than 98.6° F (37° C), then you are sick.

When the temperature of the air outside goes down to 32° F (0° C), water in the air turns to ice. This means it will snow!

What do you think?

Match the temperature to the outdoor activity.

32° F (0° C)   Skiing   82° F (28° C)
Swimming

Measuring volume

Volume is the measurement of how much space matter takes up. Liquids and some solids such as sugar can be poured and measured in measuring cups. **Graduated cylinders** and **beakers** are other tools that show how much space a liquid or solid takes up. Lines of measurement on each tool give number values for volume in ounces or cups (milliliters), or gallons (liters).

Tools for measuring volume are see-through. That way you can see the matter inside the container, as well as the numbers on the outside of it. You read the number at the very top of the matter to find the amount of volume of matter inside.

The volume of liquids and some solids is usually measured in ounces (liters). The volume of gases and some solids can be found by liquid **displacement**. Displacement is the amount of liquid that is pushed out of the way when a solid or gas is pushed down into a liquid.

The volume of this orange slice can be found by measuring the amount of water it splashes out of this full bowl of water.

What do you think?

The number value on a bottle or carton of juice tells you the volume, or how much liquid, each container holds. Which of these two containers holds more volume? Hint: The letters "oz" mean ounces and the letter "L" means liters.

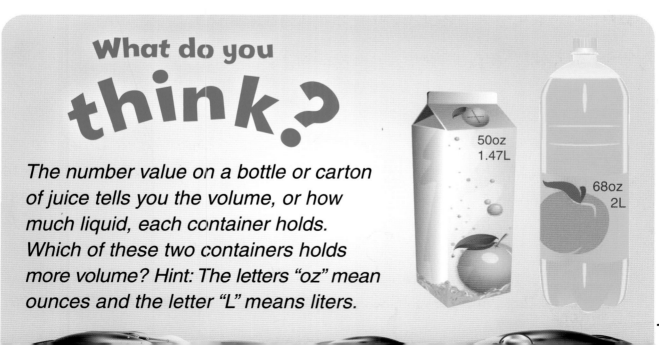

50oz
1.47L

68oz
2L

15

Measuring mass

Mass is the amount of matter in an object. All matter has mass, even a gas such as air. A heavy object has more mass than a light object. A **balance** is a tool that can measure an object's mass and compare the mass between two objects.

*You can measure mass using mass pieces, which are objects for which you know the weight. On this balance, the piggybank is on one side and the mass piece is on the other. You must keep adding more mass pieces until the two sides are **level**, or even. The amount of mass in the piggybank will be the same as the total weight of the mass pieces.*

Both the mass and weight of an object are measured in ounces and pounds (grams and kilograms). A scale is a tool that measures weight. It tells us how heavy or light things are. When you place an object in or on the scale, it gives you a number value for what the object weighs.

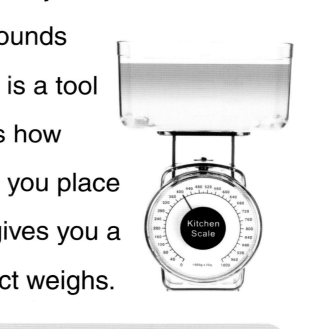

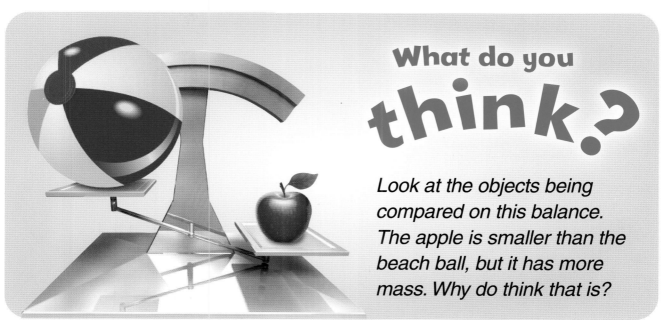

What do you think?

Look at the objects being compared on this balance. The apple is smaller than the beach ball, but it has more mass. Why do think that is?

Measuring size

A ruler is a measuring tool that measures the size of an object. Lines on a ruler show how many inches something is. Metric rulers have lines that show centimeters instead. Some rulers show inches on one side and centimeters on the other. A tape measure is longer than a ruler. It measures shapes, such as your waist, that cannot be measured with a straight-edged ruler.

Solid matter has its own shape. You can measure how tall, wide, or long a solid is. A liquid or gas does not have its own shape. Both change to fit the container they are in. You cannot measure the size of a liquid or gas.

A yardstick is three feet long. A meter stick is about the same size, but it has centimeters instead of inches.

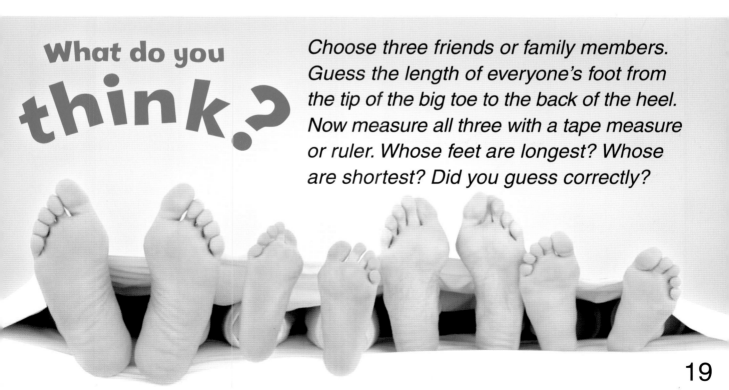

What do you think?

Choose three friends or family members. Guess the length of everyone's foot from the tip of the big toe to the back of the heel. Now measure all three with a tape measure or ruler. Whose feet are longest? Whose are shortest? Did you guess correctly?

Show your data on a graph

Scientists record data, such as measurements, using charts and graphs. Charts and graphs help organize information and make it easy for others to understand. For example, the chart below shows the height of a child at different ages.

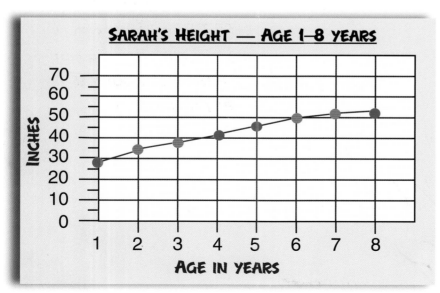

SARAH'S HEIGHT — AGE 1–8 YEARS

INCHES

AGE IN YEARS

*A **line graph** is used to show how something changes over a short or long period of time. For example, this line graph shows the height of a child over eight years.*

What are graphs?

Graphs present data using pictures, numbers, bars, lines, or dots. Graphs help people understand data and answer questions. The information recorded in a chart can be used to create a graph. Different types of graphs are used to present different types of data.

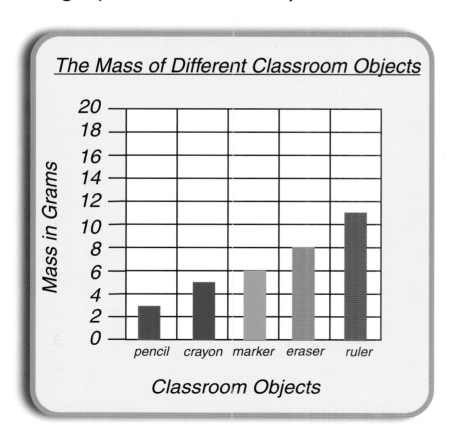

The Mass of Different Classroom Objects

A **bar graph** is used to show how things compare. This bar graph shows the mass of different objects in the classroom.

Reading a graph

This bar graph shows the temperature of the air in different locations. Use the information from the graph to answer the questions.

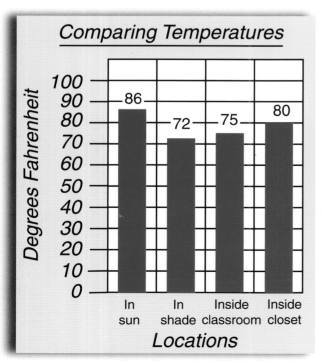

Comparing Temperatures

Degrees Fahrenheit (y-axis: 0, 10, 20, 30, 40, 50, 60, 70, 80, 90, 100)

In sun: 86
In shade: 72
Inside classroom: 75
Inside closet: 80

Locations

What do you think?

1 *Where is the temperature the highest? Why do you think this is?*

2 *Where is the best place to go when you are feeling too warm?*

3 *Find the difference between the highest temperature and the lowest temperature. Hint: Use your math skills!*

Now you try

Recreate this graph using temperatures measured in Celsius.

22

Learning more

Books

Amazing Materials (Amazing Science series) by Sally Hewitt, Crabtree Publishing, 2008.

Changing Materials (*Working with Materials* series) by Chris Oxlade, Crabtree Publishing, 2008.

Websites

www.harcourtschool.com/activity/states_of_matter
Find how particles in a solid, a liquid, or a gas behave under a virtual microscope on this website.

http://e-learningforkids.org/Courses/EN/S0602/index.html
Mr. Beaker explains the three main states of matter, and how and why they change on this fun, interactive website.

http://pbskids.org/cyberchase/math-games/poddle-weigh-in/
Have fun adding weights to a balance to find out how much a poodle weighs in this interactive cartoon game.

Glossary

Note: Some boldfaced words are defined where they appear in the book.

balance [BAL-ans] *noun* A tool that measures the mass or weight of objects

beaker [BEE-ker] *noun* A large container with a flat bottom used in a laboratory

graduated cylinders [GRAJ-oo-ey-tid SIL-in-ders] *adjective* and *noun* A series of tubes, open at one end; each tube is larger than the one before

metric system [ME-trik SIS-tuhm] *noun* A set of measurements used in most countries, especially for science

property [PROP-er-tee] *noun* A special quality or attribute that a kind of matter has.

temperature [TEMP-er-a-chur] *noun* A measure of how hot or cold something is

U.S. customary system [YOO-ESS KUHS-tuh-mer-ee SIS-tuhm] *noun* A set of measurements used in the United States

A noun is a person, place, or thing. An adjective is a word that tells you what something is like.

Index